Harpy With Benefits

A Royal Monster Girl Erotica

Cithrel

Copyright © 2023 by Cithrel

All rights reserved. No part of this publication may be reproduced, stored or transmitted in any form or by any means, electronic, mechanical, photocopying, recording, scanning, or otherwise without written permission from the publisher. It is illegal to copy this book, post it to a website, or distribute it by any other means without permission.

This novel is entirely a work of fiction. The names, characters and incidents portrayed in it are the work of the author's imagination. Any resemblance to actual persons, living or dead, events or localities is entirely coincidental.

Cithrel asserts the moral right to be identified as the author of this work.

Cithrel has no responsibility for the persistence or accuracy of URLs for external or third-party Internet Websites referred to in this publication and does not guarantee that any content on such Websites is, or will remain, accurate or appropriate.

All characters are consenting adults over the age of 18. No monsters were harmed in the making of this book.

Contents

1. Provisions   1
2. Flight   12
3. Soak   16
4. Offering   35
5. Oblige   44

About the Author   51

Join the Newsletter   52

Also by Cithrel   53

1

Provisions

The midnights in the canyon were unexpectedly frigid. One might've thought that the day's heat would've carried over, but that was not the case. Without a cloud in the sky, it left without a trace, leaving things acceptably chilly. A thicker set of robes addressed such minor grievances.

Too bad it was noon on a blistering summer day.

The sun unleashed its full might now, shimmering the sandy mounds and ridges in the distance as it became difficult to even stand in one place for too long.

At least a wind would blow through the plateau here and there, hissing in the sand as it carried away some of the heat. Sometimes she'd win the lottery, and it'd blow directly on her. That—combined with the bazaar's canopy—made things barely bearable here for a shopping trip.

Most lived in the underground capital city of Mednessa for that reason, where things were perfectly average through sun and moon, where the ground was walkably solid, where the waterways kept the populace hydrated...

...and where the harpy was a wanted criminal.

A few encounters with some traders meant Helianne would only walk through the city in chains behind a newly prosperous bounty hunter. She was hungry and poor back then, and those city merchants had plenty to go around. How much value could they put on a few forgettable sacks and barrels, anyway?

Apparently a lot.

Each failed attempt to bring her to justice raised her reward and infamy, which brought in more failed attempts and even more notoriety. It wasn't long before the harpy had quite the name, numbers, and missing mercenaries under her.

Fortunately, the shantytowns and traveling markets on Dustia's elevated outskirts cared little for bounties or outlaws. Precious metals were precious metals regardless of their origin, and each crumpled armor and weapon increased her coin, which could buy all sorts of necessities.

"Your Majesty, please slow down!" With a cart behind them, Aster and Nerine wove through the market's crowd.

Unlike their portrayals in the narrow tales passed down in the mountains of Spire, the werewolves here were shorter, less furry, politer, and more interested in exchanging goods and services than tearing out throats or carving up bellies.

And these two were more interested in servitude.

Oh, and they were also much, much cuter. Hers especially, with their matching gold chokers and pink hair that made them stick out in a crowd. Aster's hair was short, Nerine's was slightly longer, and the harpy's feathers adorned both.

The other werewolves at the market didn't seem to care that she had practically domesticated two of their kin. Then again, those two were... never mind.

However, the market-wolves *did* care about how sloppy they were at navigating the place, and that earned the three visitors plenty of glares, plentier than that time she jested they were simply humans with wolf's ears and tails. Or that time she took off in the middle of the market.

Five coins wobbled on a slightly happier shopkeeper's counter as Aster carried a pot of dye over to the cart. It creaked when he set it inside, and it creaked again as the two resumed pulling it.

For a second.

Then came a clank of forty-or-so coins for a barrel of water. After it landed in the wagon, Aster braced himself against the wagon's side and panted a few times.

Helianne's attention was already elsewhere, her head having turned to the stalls behind her.

She might have rotated a bit beyond the range of how far heads were expected to turn, but how else was she supposed to get a good look at those blankets without wasting time spinning around?

Paleness cut through the shopkeeper's dark skin as the harpy's head turned back to her, and she turned even paler after Helianne flashed the werewolf a fidgeting smile.

Helianne rubbed her wings together. Hmmm... what else did she need today? Oh yeah, some Mednessite staples! Thankfully, they sold them here too, otherwise the queen's food stores would've stayed empty of such wonderments.

But first, eleven more coins for perfume.

Aster reached for the delicate, citrusy bottle on the counter, but Nerine was faster. The wolf girl pocketed it and tousled his hair with her free hand as she stuck out her tongue.

With clothes to the north, trinkets to the east, artisans to the south, and food to the west, everything was so organized here. As for the market's center, that held all the odd things, like drugs, toys, mercenaries, massages, and Helianne.

Aster and Nerine stopped their bickering as their queen eyed the rows and rows of food stalls in the distance.

A rainbow of aromas greeted the harpy as she skipped her way to the western quarter of the market. Sweet scents ambushed her from one direction, spice and citrus from another, and the nostalgic scent of baked goods from... that way!

Her mouth watered as she hopped into the bakery's short line. Behind the counter, countless werewolves and the occasional dust elf toiled away in the kitchen. Some powered the gristmill, others kneaded dough, a few watched the ovens, and one managed the counter.

A welcoming heat emanated from there, and its scented glow met her more and more while the queue thinned.

They specialized in biscuits made of equal parts locusts and wheat. Perhaps a thrifty farmer of ancient times wanted to make the most out of a plagued harvest, only for the daring dish to take off in popularity. In Mednessa, they dipped them in sauces, mixed them into stews, and crumbled them back into dough for bread. Fancier citizens stuffed them with meat and cheese, or honey and jam. Or so she'd heard.

That was what living in a place with barely any livestock did to people.

Sure, there were lobsters, oysters, and the occasional fish from the ocean, but no one could stomach those slimy creatures for long, and they'd last for a second in the sandy heat. A baked-thrice biscuit stayed good for pretty much forever, and was plump, spiced, nutty, and ready to be dunked in some delicious—

"Miss, miss? Are you ready to order?"

After a twitch, she skipped to the counter.

"Yes, I'll have... fifty." Actually, how many hardtacks did she need? The traveling merchants would leave in a few days, and who knew when they'd come back? A few weeks? A few months? Her eyes darted around as she stroked her neck with the tip of her wing. Three mouths to feed. Kind of. And supplemented by a couple of lobsters. "Sixty." Ugh, anything but those... maybe just a few fish. "No wait, one hundred!"

The clerk cocked his head and frowned. "One hundred *what*?"

Oh yeah, they sold more than one thing here.

"Sorry, *biscuits*."

"And will that be here or—"

"To go!" The harpy raised her wing high, blasting the counter with grainy wind and knocking off a few papers. "Sorry again."

The werewolf coughed as he disappeared under the counter. After some shuffling, he reappeared and reorganized the counter before going behind a pile of biscuits and baskets in the middle of the kitchen. After a few, some, and then a lot of clacks, he emerged with a large basket. It hissed against the dusty floor as he struggled to bring it to her.

Her talons tapped the ground. "Umm... I think you're short by three biscuits."

He gave her an awful look before muttering something that she'd rather not pay attention to. Come on, they'd missed seven last time around, despite being able to make change for a gold tooth. If the biscuits weren't so good, why she'd...

Calm, she needed to be calm. Helianne closed her eyes and took a deep breath. At least her subjects were at her side now.

The clerk returned with the same basket, presumably filled with three more biscuits.

Even with the strength of three werewolves, that thing left them dizzy and trickling after it slammed into the cart.

"Thank you!" said the three of them, a bit off-sync.

The clerk said nothing and waved to the next customer. Wow, that line sure got long while she was called up. Was she too rude when correcting him, or did she order a strange number of biscuits? Or what if she was supposed to tip the clerk for helping them lift the basket into the cart? Was that customary? And why did he smile at that customer, but not her?!

She needed a nap.

Maybe he'd forget about her after a few weeks, but then again, she was the only harpy in the whole desert. Probably. She had to have been the only one who'd visited this caravan regularly, and at the very least, the only pink-haired one.

Maybe they ought to not dye their hair for a while.

Regardless, it was all over, and she could now retire to her dwelling with her much more considerate subjects.

This time, Helianne was just slightly ahead of Aster and Nerine as they left the bazaar. It wasn't because of that interaction with the shopkeeper. Okay, it kind of was, but the cart was also heavier and a prime target for a hungry crook, or one with a boring hair color.

Not to mention she felt bad for running off earlier.

It was also because there were more people around. The tall harpy wrapped her wings around her body like a cloak as she squeezed through the tangle of perky ears and tails.

Her eyes snagged on a barren spot in the crowd.

A small pack of werewolves cheered in its center, and the mob cheered back. Unlike the others dressed in cloth, this group was equipped with hide armor and spears, and the smallest of the bunch wore a bandolier of smoky flasks.

"...our raid on Mednessa's outpost was a success, and our spoils..." The tall wolfess's voice trailed off into the crowd's.

Yawn. Just a bunch of marauders giving everyone here a bad name, including her. Today it'd be the capital, and tomorrow it'd be their lair. Guess it didn't matter for the raider-wolves, since reputation mattered little to those who'd be gone in a few days. But what ends could've justified—

"Who among you desires..." The wolfess held up a rusted telescope. "...*this*?!"

Her, absolutely. It wasn't like a Mednessite would have grieved for a few missing trinkets, anyway.

The crowd let out a collective snarl.

"Not this garbage again!" said one of them.

Long had she yearned to soar high and gaze upon the world beneath in clear sight. While the former was always available to her, the shine and grind of the desert's sun and sand had worn her farsight into muddy streaks for the latter.

"I'll take it! How much?" Helianne jumped and waved at the bandit. As the tallest one there, the harpy already had plenty of attention, and that gesture earned her the glance and silence of everyone else.

"It's free, didn't you hear?" The werewolf cocked her head at the harpy before raising the spyglass. "All yours, miss."

She was losing energy left and right from all these blunders.

Helianne's magic plucked the telescope from the werewolf's hand into the cart. Damn her habits. Now the crowd was poking her feathers, jingling her jewelry, and asking if she was open for work.

It was time to leave.

The queen and her servants fled the market, literally leaving their hecklers in the dust. Their paces and breaths calmed as they reached the opposite side of the plateau.

The sun had yet to budge from the middle of the sky, but the breeze was much stronger now, leaving the three hot but mostly unbothered despite the loss of the bazaar's roofs. Provided they kept moving, losing shade meant little to the exiles who'd spent years living on the desert surface. It also helped that they all wore pale outfits. Matching ones, of course.

They reached the first of many bridges connecting plateau to plateau, except this one wasn't there anymore. A few tattered ropes leading into the black below were all that remained of it. Maybe a powerful gust of wind or a heavy cart took it out during their time at the market?

The harpy drew her nictitating membranes over her eyes, turning her surroundings a blurry gray. A breach was nothing a winged monster like her couldn't conquer, and her servants knew it as well. Scaling the harpy's height, Nerine ended up on Helianne's back, while Aster held onto the queen's torso and waist.

Now all she had to do was get a running start—oh, and levitate the cart. While it floated in the air, she stepped back from the rift and stuck her tongue out to the side. After a deep breath, her walk became a run, and finally a sprint. Sand stormed behind her by the time she neared the edge.

Then she hurled herself, the clinging werewolves, and the wagon into the cleft. Helianne flapped on the descent, slowing their fall until they were hovering in place. Sweat trickled down her chin as her motions smeared, and soon they all rose.

Except for the biscuits, whoops.

That poor, heavy basket jostled and shifted from the cart's tilt, and their rise had given it just enough bounce for it to go overboard. While hovering in place, she expected a thud after the darkness of the rift consumed it, but there was no response.

She shifted her angle and swooped them across the chasm. As they landed on the other side, the harpy and her freight made a whispered skid across the ground.

Aster dropped from the harpy and ran to the cliff's edge, peering down before sighing. "There goes dinner."

"If *you* were the one cooking." Nerine fell down too, flicking her tail as she put her hands on her hips. "Corpulence or crumbs, Her Majesty's head chef shall create a worthy dish!"

"Or we can just head back there." With twitching ears, Aster pointed back to the wavy market in the distance. "We're not destitute."

The two werewolves neared their queen with expectant faces and quivering lips.

The harpy swept them up in a hug, smothering their adorably heated bodies in her feathers. Impartial as she was, today she'd unfortunately have to side with Nerine.

Encountering that clerk a second time today? No thanks, she'd rather give him a night to either forget about her or give his judgment a break. It'd also be an interesting change to eat something different.

"Let's do that tomorrow. Your queen needs rest," she whispered.

After the two returned to the wagon and heaved the pulling bar over their shoulders, the wolf girl smirked at Aster and he frowned back.

If there was another broken bridge, they'd have to cross it the grounded way. Helianne stumbled into the cart, adding herself to the cargo as the world spun around her. As the harpy exhaled deep, she shaded her face with a bittered wing.

Physical strain was only half of it.

The werewolves and cart were light compared to the weight of her obligations. A mistimed flap or a sneeze would've sent them down the rift with that basket. Would she recover? Would they lose their grip on her in the process? Then, would she float them in time or—

Helianne sighed.

All these burdens, but it was worth it for such company. What else could keep her going in this barren place? Maybe the food and that peculiar orcess, but those weren't as dependable or cute as two followers at her beck and call.

This was her fortune and her people, all under her kingdom to preserve, as things should've been.

The rhythmic rumbles of her servants' footsteps and the night's facsimile from her wings drifted the harpy to a well-deserved rest.

Putting her assumptions of the shopkeeper away, her thoughts turned to Aster and Nerine, and how their fates ended up weaving together.

2

Flight

Sharing an eastern border with the desert was Spire, an orange, fogbound land buried beneath countless stone pillars that speared through the clouds. Only harpies could soar through the thicket of rocks and forage the bounties high and low.

Abundance and safety encouraged alliances, and alliances coalesced under a sovereign, offering stability and order. With their few foes driven out of the stone forest, it became the perfect home for them.

Almost all of them, for twin sisters emerged from the queen's egg. One was majestic, silver-tongued, and dignified, and one was not. So what purpose did the peasant-sister serve, other than potentially sparking heresy against the crown?

The guards allowed her no audience and belongings that night of exile.

Arrows rushed past her from her now-enemies as she fled the palace grounds, and a frantic, feather-shedding dive off of Spire's highest point turned into a glide into the neighboring desert.

Perhaps they intended for her to die that day. The arrows were meant to injure, sparing the conscience of those who nocked their bows, while the desert and the lack of supplies delivered the finishing blow.

But Helianne was of a harpy of magical blood, and in a land of normals, she was the apex predator. Merchant caravans, bandits, and the occasional animal just couldn't stand a chance against her.

She survived out of spite at first, but there was a growing need for something more. Erstwhile or not, she still considered herself royalty, and what was a queen without a domain?

It didn't take long for her to be nestled in a cave brimming with treasure, and for tales of her to spread through the desert. Furs, jewelry, food... she truly had anything and everything.

Except some camaraderie.

That orcess was okay, kind of. Whenever they'd cross paths, they'd duel over something: an abandoned cart, a merchant trail, whoever had the best fashion sense, or whatever else that greenie came up with at the moment.

And even though the harpy always lost, the victorious orc would always split things evenly. Perhaps the glory of combat was what she truly desired. Typical orc.

Battle cries, however, were not conversation, and Helianne was getting sick of talking to her waterside reflection for days on end.

It was an amber evening in the desert when the harpy skipped home from a newly discovered werewolf bazaar. It held quite the variety of goods, and she made a mental note to bring something tradeable next time. Pillaging had made her quite the fortune by now, so there was no need to be wrathful toward another group of outsiders.

That rule did not extend to intruders, especially sloppy ones who didn't even bother clearing out their tracks. Twin footprints marked the sacred ground at her kingdom's gates, and the faint shuffling of sand echoed from within.

The cave plunged beneath the surface before keeping a gentle incline that went on and on. As the harpy delved deeper with tranquil steps, she passed the usual lantern-lit piles of crumpled metal and jewelry, interestingly undisturbed by the supposed treasure hunters.

After the treasury was the kitchen.

Just what did they want from her, if not her most valuable possessions? Pots and pans? Spices? Her?

Or... food?

Two werewolves were sitting on the ground with their backs to her. While their tails wagged, they ferally chewed in front of a sack of bread. Further ahead was her pantry, which went untouched, save for an ajar crate.

Helianne crept closer as she held her breath.

The female werewolf sniffed the air, and the male followed.

Sand and crumbs flew everywhere as the two sprung onto their quaking feet, facing the harpy. Fear drenched their faces for a few moments before widening into fury, and each werewolf drew a knife before rushing her.

Her kitchen's knives.

They must've been new or desperate. Also, weren't those the two on that wanted poster in the bazaar, with a petty meal voucher on each of their heads?

Helianne closed her brown eyes as time slowed. When they reopened, they glowed violet, and the werewolves' faces rebounded to fear and flight, but it was too late.

A matching violet mist surrounded the two of them, and soon they were floating in the air, stilled against their wills. Their weapons clanged against the sandy rock beneath as their hands loosened.

The pair must've known who she was now, for after a few moments of straining, they yelled for help.

The harpy kept watch on both sides of the tunnel, but no one came.

Screaming for help turned into indecipherable pleading as she lifted off pieces of their tattered clothes to get a thorough look. Their gurgling bellies were hollow and their ribcages were prominent, which matched the scarcity in their arms and legs.

By the time the harpy's eyes returned to their bony faces, they were scrunched up and dripping with tears.

Two nobodies at the edge of society, seeking sanctuary and company.

Sounded familiar.

Her smile took the two werewolves back at first, but after her soothing voice offered them abundance and renewal, they shared in her grin, first faintly and then obviously.

When her magic ceased, they returned the knives and food to their proper places before being seated at a table, as eating on the floor was beneath a queen's servants.

Aster and Nerine went through so much bread and wine that night.

3

Soak

The familiar scent of warm stew and steam kindled Helianne from her dream, and her eyes opened to the ceiling of the cave. In her deep sleep, they had carried her into a corner with all kinds of furs and fabrics piled across the floor.

It sort of resembled the eyries her kind would build during their early days in Spire. Except the desert outcasts' take on it was way better, of course. There were no pointy sticks nor sticky driderwebs to ruin one's fall and rise, and there were no smelly carcasses laid about.

The harpy rose, sweeping a wing across her face and stretching her legs with a crack. Aided by the lanterns on the cave walls, she followed the scent into the kitchen.

"You're stirring too fast." Nerine crossed her arms as she watched Aster work the pot. "Now, too slow." She spotted the harpy and her tail flicked.

The wolf boy managed a few more stirs before Nerine yanked the wooden paddle out of his hands. "Hey!"

"Why don't you go bathe Mistress instead?" The wolf girl pointed at Helianne.

He threw his hands up in the air as his ears fluttered like little wings. "Why don't *you* go bathe her so I can learn to cook?"

"Maybe if you were the one eating." She flashed him a toothy smile. "I don't think Her Majesty wants to eat burned soup again."

After a jaw-tensed pause, the wolf boy sighed and slacked his shoulders as he approached the harpy. "This way, Mistress."

While holding the end of one of Helianne's wings, he led her deeper into the cave.

The atmosphere turned from steamy to arid and back to steamy as they wove and ducked through several columns of stone. The growing warmth meant they were close.

A massive pool laid at the back of the cave.

Bubbles streamed from cracks in its bed, giving the water a perfect, effervescent heat. While the water was calm near the edge, the deep end of the pool was splashing and swirling as the water entered and left from somewhere unseen. Traces of moss padded the surrounding rock, providing their feet with a ruglike luxury.

Not even the highest point in Spire had such amenities.

"You'll learn eventually." Helianne ran her wings across the wolf boy's head. "Remember when I was cooking for you two?"

"Yeah..." He stared at the ground. "...but since then, she's picked it up faster than me."

"And you're better at bathing me." Helianne flexed a small projection on the edge of her wing. "She can cook and you can clean. Shouldn't a queen's servants be specialized?"

Aster rubbed one of his ears. "That's true, but cooking just seems more dignified. And fun. Maybe it's become too routine for me..."

While an idea stewed in the corner of her mind, Helianne kneeled and folded her wings, allowing the werewolf to disrobe her.

Her hair was much shorter, but now it ran down to her thighs. One benefit to having attendants was being able to trade practicality for regality.

As for her body, it remained the same throughout the years. Of blue blood, she was enduringly majestic from top to bottom, from her queenly breasts, to her thighs that matched her wings in fluffiness, to her polished and painted talons.

Having undressed her so many times, he must've memorized every button, strap, and hole in the harpy's clothes by now. As such, he always looked elsewhere when undressing her, perhaps also out of politeness or to banish any wicked thoughts.

The towering harpy had no shame watching the werewolf undress himself. Not that he could ever call her out on it. What a royal privilege.

Aster looked even cuter naked, especially with the lean muscle that had grown on him. It was a considerable recovery from the pile of bones he was before.

Even when he was clothed, there were just so many things to stare at, like how his ears and tail moved compared to his co-servant. Side by side, their motions would slowly synchronize until they'd notice. Then they'd break the rhythm, and the entire process would start anew. The harpy could watch those two for hours...

"Mistress?" The wolf boy was already in the pool.

Ah yes, the bath.

His bushy tail was wrapped around his waist like a skirt, keeping him decent. It was only fair, considering how her feathers covered everything below her hips.

Passing their clothes on the ground, Helianne stepped over the damp edge of the pool before squatting and lying on her back.

The water's depth covered her halfway as she spread her limbs and blanketed the area in her generous wings. Waves ebbed and flowed against her, soaking her feathers as the harpy's hair drifted over her head.

Aster rummaged through a chest at the pool's edge, withdrawing a few flasks before rubbing their contents onto the thin fur on his hands and arms. When things were thoroughly bubbly, he scooted over to her.

She closed her eyes and took a deep breath. It was more to relax than to avoid tasting or seeing soap—he had only made that mistake once.

The werewolf's fingers ran through her hair and into her scalp, dislodging the sand and grime there as he hummed a tune. His filed-down claws grazed deep against her skin, leaving a crisp sensation in their wake as they scratched away itches she didn't even know she had.

Her talons scrawled into the stone beneath her, and the resulting vibrations tensed her legs.

She had a servant attending to her, the water was a perfect temperature, the soap's citrusy scent graced her lungs, and the pool's flow created a divine soundscape. So why was her body still so twitchy?

The clerk.

Ordering so many biscuits, and being so annoying with the quantity... Out of all the unruly customers he had that day, she must've been the strangest one he didn't smile for.

What if the other shopkeepers were sharing notes on bad customers?

A pink harpy and her two pets making a mockery of werewolves everywhere. They'd ban her from the shop. No, the entire bazaar, and not just her, but every harpy!

She'd have to forage or rob people again. And there were two servants to reinitiate into thievery after all the work put into freeing them from such vices...

"All done. Now for your wings."

There wasn't much of a difference between being bathed and being soothingly massaged. Except for today, where it might as well have been just a bath given how shaken she was.

Maybe she ought to think about other things. Like Aster, who was meticulously washing her plumage.

What a cutie, doing things exactly as she had taught him. Wake and wind had sullied her feathers, and each one had to be restored between his fingers until the water dewed at its surface once more.

The squeak of his soaped pads against her feathers vibrated deep into the quills, loosening long-untouched knots while it whisked away the grains of filth.

He repeated the process on her other wing.

With his tail wagging and his tongue stuck out, it was obvious that he enjoyed washing her. Perhaps that dispelled the notion that such acts were boring and lowly. There were barbules to realign, feathers to fluff, and oil to knead in.

There was glory in being the only werewolf to know about harpy preening.

Her wings took the longest to groom, but the rest of her was also a challenge, like her sensitive neck and shoulders. It was a battle fought with giggles and flails where a pinned wing meant a thrashing talon, and a pinned talon meant a thrashing wing.

Four limbs against four. Being lathered up made things hard for him, and droplets and suds splashed everywhere as the werewolf fell onto the harpy.

Aster's tail unfurled as it always did when he was surprised, and his waist met hers as his head met her royal bosom with a wet slap. His body was like an iron against her, especially his face, which nicely warmed her chest.

He lay frozen against her now, solely blinking while his heart leaped against her.

Looking away could only do so much for the wolf boy, and he wasn't free of wicked thoughts, either.

Something hard nestled into the firm feathers that guarded her crotch, and every few seconds his hips made the faintest of prods against that area, unraveling that barrier bit by bit. Matching his breaths against her chest were throbs that first warmed and then dampened her flesh as he drove his heat into her.

Just before his thrusts could part her deepest, fluffiest feathers, he gasped and pulled away. A trail connected their groins for a peculiarly long moment before the werewolf's tail coiled around his waist once more. While her feathers had darkened overall from the water, the spot where they had touched had a darker, stickier shade.

Aster's eyes followed the harpy's to that spot, and at once he was kneeling between her legs and washing her again. Water spilled from his hands as he poured it over her crotch.

His breaths were swifter than usual, and his ears were practically fanning his head.

"You didn't finish washing my—"

His ears stood straight up. "Right, I'll get to that next!"

"—neck and body."

Helianne closed her eyes as a boiled breath escaped her. Anyone having their groin prodded and then scrubbed like that would've had similar reactions. Beneath the feathers, the harpy's own heat seeped out of her before being washed away.

His nose had to have known, given it was the same one that had detected her during their first encounter. Just what would Aster do once he picked up that scent?

Apparently, try to hide his sniffing while tightening his tail around his hips. Although she couldn't see anything there, his belly stuttered in its rise and fall so obviously, and there was a certain momentum to his swaying.

That was all he did when his hands were on her neck, but things became more interesting once he got to the part beneath.

Even when looking away, he had always gotten fussed when washing her bosom, but today his hands were fretting way more than usual. After a few shaky attempts, he clenched his jaw, allowing his fingers to finish cleaning the rim of her breasts.

Aster moved onto their fronts, squeezing each one still with one hand as his other's bare palm squeaked on its surface. When he wrung her nipples clean by gripping and rolling them between his finger pads, the sensation traveled deep into her chest, making her shiver and gasp under her breath as those nubs hardened.

He'd shudder every so often as well, dripping liquid from under his skirted tail into the pool. It fell far too slow to have been water.

Nothing extra happened with her legs and talons as he picked through their tough scales for dirt and ran a whetstone across them. Just some expected oozing shudders. A soft, bushy tail wound and fidgeting so tightly against a groin would've done that to anyone.

A folded towel spared her delicate breasts from the unforgiving rock while he worked on her opposite side. Strangely, he hesitated more on the harpy's back than on her rear or tailfeathers. Years of flight must've made those back muscles and shoulder blades look heavenly.

"All d-done!" he said with an exhale. Pulling her wing until she was standing, he led her out of the pool. Tried to anyway.

The beaming harpy wouldn't budge. "I believe it's your turn."

"M-me? I washed already. When you were sleeping." His ears flopped. "It won't be needed."

"Over here." Sitting at the pool's edge where its shallow depth turned deep, Helianne waved at him. "My soap and dirt's all over you."

The werewolf's hands gripped his tail as he bumbled toward her. "Nerine is waiting for us! Don't want dinner to get cold, do we?"

"It'll be a few extra minutes." The harpy's magic coiled around Aster before pulling him over with no resistance. "Cover your face."

"Okay..."

His tail shivered against his groin as he brought his hands up to his head, pinching his nose with one and shielding his eyes with the other.

She floated him to the deeper half of the pool as his toe claws skimmed the water's surface. A wrinkle of her nose sunk him, and another wrinkle brought him up for a breath. Up and down he plunged, splashing water and foaming traces of soap at a safe distance from his queen.

Aster was shiny when she pulled him back over.

"Hmmm, still dirty…" The tip of her wing scaled his trembling leg as he wiped his eyes. "…here."

She lied. He was clean there. At least until her feathers left. Aster's oozing, firming length was visible for a second before his hands rushed to cover it.

Only for her eyebrows to raise as her magic bound his arms over his head. His tail tried covering him next, and she bound that too. Grunting, he twisted his waist and neck, putting on a nostalgic show before his body relaxed in defeat.

A blush cut through his brown skin, looking as obvious as ever as his lip quivered. Helianne's eyes shifted between his eyes and his member while her smile grew wide.

Little by little, her magic worked him, shlicking the skin back and forth on his glans until his length stood proudly. Then she stopped and leaned in closer as he dribbled into the water.

She sniffed the air. It was certainly a werewolf's musk.

He was twitching harder now, and an impressive spurt would've defiled her face had she not intercepted it with her telekinesis. The harpy pulled back and gave Aster a demanding look.

The werewolf sucked in a breath. "The... the water! It was rubbing against me so much and-and-and—"

Poor Aster, always having to admire her in his peripheral vision. She spread her legs until there was enough room for a tailed monster to sit and plopped him there, back against her front. The werewolf's head split her breasts, and she peered between them to see him.

His ears were wagging when he gazed upward. As was his tail, whose base unintentionally flitted over her groin's feathers. The harpy's curiosity never ceased, and the wolf boy covered himself with his hands after noticing.

"Does this always happen when you bathe me?" Her magic jostled the fingers over his member. Although she could only examine his eyes now, that might've been a worse fate.

He swallowed repeatedly as his ears and tail stilled. "Yes, Mistress. You're very..." His eyes darted away for a moment. "...elegant."

Sheer sincerity from a well-trained servant.

"Is that why you humped my crotch when you fell on me?"

His hands gripped her thighs instead of his, but they did not correct themselves, as he had more embarrassing things to worry about. "I... you... y-you were *really* silky. And my body... I-it moved on its own!"

"That's okay."

"I'm... What?!"

Ahhh... that swishing tail felt so... interesting.

"It's been that time for you two for a while now. No surprise you'd fancy something better than your hands," said Helianne.

Her wing wrapped around his abdomen, and his stomach clenched before softening.

The werewolf hugged her wing. "You're so understanding, Mistress!"

"The last decent Spirian." She rubbed his belly as her wings closed in, causing her bare upper arms to squeeze her breasts inward against his temples. "My servant, which aspect of your queen do you adore the most?"

"Y-your... your...!" He could barely answer through his laughter, and so she eased her motions, and the words sprayed from his lungs. "W-w-wings!"

A refined desire.

"Not surprising that my dearest servant would appreciate Her Majesty's feathers." The harpy stroked her other wing across his face a few times and he squirmed out of her bosom. No longer flattened against her, his tail skimmed her loins and front, hardening her nipples and retreating her abdomen. "It's no gift. Your queen expects something in return, too."

The position was awkward, and time was not on their side, but Helianne would make it work. Her magic guided Aster's hands behind him and into her crotch. When his fingers probed through the rigid coating of feathers into the fluffy goodness beneath, his digits recoiled for a moment before resting there.

The werewolf's tail stood up straight as his digits fidgeted. "Mistress, I've never... I don't know how..."

"Think of it like a focused massage." The violet fog dug his fingers through her downy layer and against her tender flesh. One hand's delving was shallow, ending up above the other, which pierced her slightly deeper.

"Feel that fold and that nub with this one?" She squeezed his left hand. "Keep your fingers there."

"And this one?" Her magic coiled around his right hand's fingers. "Thrust and flex them this way." Helianne exhaled deeply as her entrance received his fingertips.

Aster kept his claws trimmed, and with his pads in contact with the ceiling of her tunnel...

"There'll b-be something rough at the top when you're a bit more in. Rub that spot. Oh, and follow my pace," said the harpy.

"You're so patient, Mistress! I'll do my best."

It didn't seem fair that while his hands served her, her wings did not reciprocate. Her breasts rested on his shoulders as she leaned forward to even the scales.

One wing shielded his front, pulling him back slightly to give her a better view. For a second, his hands contemplated retreating from their royal posts. As her other wing approached his hips, his legs spread, offering her yet another generous view of his length.

The longer she stared, the harder he became.

His member bounded with his heartbeat and breaths, while his slit oozed a thin liquid that gathered between the two halves of his glans. It met the rim of his retracted foreskin before dripping into the pool.

A shame she'd dirty her feathers after Aster spent so much time cleaning them. But maybe he actually wanted to sully those regal wings of hers and then be commanded to renew them like the dutiful servant he was.

And at least it'd come out easier than the sand. Probably. Maybe.

She'd find out soon enough.

An initial poke of the harpy's wing against his tip shivered his spine and retreated his neck and shoulders closer to her chest. As the wing over his torso tightened to stay his fidgeting, a strand connected his shaft's head with her spoiled feather before breaking on his next throb.

Magic gathered around his tip, dragging his foreskin back all the way to give her feathers full access to that precious head of his.

Each dab upon his slit produced more and more fidgeting, and soon his ooze beaded her wingtip. It collected so copiously that the strand connecting them no longer broke, linking the queen to her servant as it thickened on every prod.

Her magic tapped his nose. "Aren't you forgetting something?"

"Sorry Mistress, it feels so good..."

The harpy knew of his pads' texture from their bathing, but now they felt so smooth, being velvety against her clit as his fingers circled her. The other set squeaked and vibrated against her interior flesh as it pumped in and out of her, making her breathing catch up to the werewolf's.

Cupping her feathers against the head of his shaft, she mirrored his motions, circling him as his fingers did to her nub and special spot. Her feathers squished and slicked against his cock as she worked them across his shaft, matching the pace of his fingers.

A foggy heat emanated from their trickling fluids, glazing the atmosphere.

Their essences cut through the scents of her prior bathing. First it was a tinge of feathery citrus, and then it was an earthen flood that was unexpected from such a thin liquid. The werewolf swallowed every so often, perhaps sensing more of it than she could.

As his fingers drained her hole, Helianne brought her wing to his cock's side and ran her feathers lengthwise. With how they were aligned, the smooth feathers caught him on every thrust, dragging the head of his shaft down into her much softer and messier down.

She pushed him deeper, and when he was bottomed out against the base of her quills, his rear would come off the ground a little and he'd make adorable thrusts into the fleecy thicket, staining it with his warmth. She'd ruffle her wings at that time, matching his thrusts as he loosed into her with soft, shivering growls.

The harpy's innermost plumes lacked waterproofing, so his pre nestled deep, wicking down her barbs and staining her skin. She made a mental note to have Aster scrub that area more thoroughly later.

Soft growls turned to gasps as he lost all subtlety. They'd pull away simultaneously, dragging his length out of her gripping down and contour feathers at twice the speed. Then they'd rejoin in the middle, piercing his length into her wing and misaligning plenty of feathers.

The first few attempts were rough, but eventually his musk trickled out of her feathers, and their efforts smoothed as her feathers and his loin shined with werewolf essence.

His tongue dangled from his mouth, and she smelled mint on his exhales. A few more strokes and his body froze until it was just the shivering of his tail and ears and nothing else.

Caked in sweat, her idle wing crackled as she peeled it from his torso. Helianne lowered it, sandwiching his member between the back of one wing and the front of the other.

By now, his tail and back were pressed up tight against her body, and his hands had abandoned their posts, instead gripping onto her thighs for dear life. From the harpy leaning down, his head sunk deep between her breasts, blinding him while his breaths fogged her cleavage from the inside out.

Smiling, Helianne breathed steam through her nose as her own heat dewed her loin feathers. Unsatisfied rested the nethers of one who wore a crown, but her servant's quivers and moans made it all worth it.

Provided there was an equally unrequited offering in the future, of course.

She raised and lowered her wings, first in lockstep with each other and then in alternating motions. The closer wing's strokes started out so clean and rough, but it didn't take long for his heat to grease that one as well.

Helianne rocked her wings back and forth. Sometimes his length would slip between the feathers of the one in front, other times the back one, and sometimes it'd remain perfectly between the two as she buffeted his member.

Shlicks and swooshes echoed in the cave as she worked him into a bubbly, twitching mess. Restricted in motion, his tail throbbed instead, and his panting tongue dripped saliva all over the inside of her breasts.

His claws dove into her thigh feathers as his muffled voice vibrated her bosom. "M-Mistress, it-it's c-c-coming...!"

That voice of his really was the cutest.

Aided by his ample fluids, she worked her wings into a blur as she closed the space around his shaft. He hardened completely as he marked the surface of her wings with the first two ropes. Then, she angled her wings on the down thrust and forced him between her feathers again.

Her feathers flexed and vibrated as he penetrated the tangle of down within her wings, and a continuous, trembling spurt flooded the space where quills met skin while the werewolf growled and humped, as if he couldn't hold off his instincts.

The watery deluge worked into her skin and filled her hollowed bones with quaking heat. More spurts followed with hotter and hotter offerings that spread through her down before dripping down her outer feathers.

While the essence dripped onto his thighs, his tail had finally escaped its sweaty prison. Its tip unwittingly teased the underside of her breasts, pushing laughter through her lips as a tremor ran up her spine. Meanwhile, his ears pulsed in tandem with his body and shaft.

Time passed as his stirring weakened, and eventually, he came to a sighing, relaxed stop. The werewolf's eyes were closed as he made soft purrs against her breasts, and his back sunk further into her front.

Must've been relaxing for him. Too relaxing for one who had forgotten his duties.

Embracing him higher, she pinned his upper half against her, leaving him in the dark as his breaths doused her cleavage. Aster was essentially an ornament in a feathered dress as she shuffled her wings upward, exposing his member, but nothing above that.

The harpy's eyes glowed while she gazed at his diminishing length. Moments later, magic whirled around him before it gathered and slipped into his entrance. As his legs beat the edge of the pool and strewed water everywhere, his cock firmed.

What a journey her violet made within him! After rushing through his length, it made a loop before cascading into his jewels. Her magic vibrated and churned there, diffusing into the lingering seed as his member pulsed.

As nothing shot out, Aster made a shivering, muffled roar as his hands shuffled in the labyrinth of feathers, desperately trying to reach his poor sack. Tightening her hug put an end to that, and he stilled in response.

Although the sound was more of overstimulation than of any pain, she still might've been a bit too rough on the poor wolf boy.

Good. Discipline ought to be harmless, yet memorable.

When her talons curled into a ball, his sex rumbled and quaked while her magic reversed its journey. He stiffened and softened repeatedly, shooting out nothing. Finally, with her mist's egress came ropes and ropes of his milky deluge, which swirled in the air.

The werewolf climaxed again and again as she drew all of his seed out, creating quite the sizable mass over the water. He had never roared nor clenched so many times before. Echoing throughout the cave and overlapping against itself, his voice seemed as infinite as his lust.

Which wasn't very infinite at all. Like before, his ropes thinned into strings, and a pained yelp followed the shedding of a final droplet of come.

When the harpy stilled her magic, she couldn't help but take deep draws through her nose. Having a bunch of lycanthrope seed in the air strangely smelled kind of good. A bit of it was dirty, but an excess amount made things smell like a sodden forest after some rain. The faint scent of citrus made things even better.

Her mouth was definitely not spitty. Nope. Not at all. A queen would never consider such depraved acts, even if it was just a slightly thicker form of water. Differing only in that it was a bit salty too. Or... sweet or bitter or spicy. She wouldn't know, of course.

Helianne gawked at the swirling seed as she sent it far, far back into the deep end of the pool. After ceasing her magic, his seed splashed into the water, ribboning it with white for a few seconds before fading into clarity.

Prying her wings from his sticky body, she freed her captive as a chill rushed in where there was once heat. Aster looked really spent as he inhaled and exhaled deeply.

Her feathers were a mess, as was the entirety of her werewolf. Helianne's magic was limited, and the werewolf's reserves were abundant on all fronts. A few particularly explosive climaxes had seeded his loins and thighs, while drool had stained his neck and chest, worsening the sweat already present.

Helianne's magic poked him in the nose, tensing him. "Her Majesty will overlook this... insubordination this time."

Aster jumped as he met her downward stare.

"Sorry Mistress, it—"

"Felt good being fully embraced by your queen?" Helianne's half-lidded eyes and smile calmed his expression. "There's no doubt in that, but your mistress has some doubt in your reciprocity. What say you, my faithful servant?"

The pool's hypnotic bubbling and streaming returned while he searched the corners of his eyes for an answer.

Eventually, the scent of stew became increasingly apparent in the air, making for an odd smell.

"While you're busy not making Her Majesty come, her f-food's getting cold!" At the edge of the pool, Nerine's arms were crossed as she soaked her feet. "A lot of work went into putting our sc-scraps and crumbs to good use, y-you know?"

By the look of her faint blush, flustered face, and restless legs, she must've been here for a while. Just how long did they take? Was it nighttime already? Living in a cave had its blessings, but there were also curses, like not being able to tell the time.

And while she had directed her quip at Aster, Helianne was the reason they were 'bathing' for so long. Wasting her dutiful servant-cook's skills made more of the harpy's energy leave her.

Helianne whispered into the petrified werewolf's ears. "Your redemption will begin with getting your queen ready for supper."

4

Offering

A few shared dunks in the deep end cleansed Helianne and Aster once more before they followed Nerine into the kitchen and dining room, err... section of the cave.

"Your fingers! Her Majesty's drawing out all your come and you decide to offer her... your fingers!" Nerine's giggling finally escaped her hand. "I bet you couldn't even find her clit."

Hard to believe that these two had mutually agreed to rob her.

"I did! With some help." Aster glanced at the harpy while his fingers ran across his tail. "Then I... umm... It was distractingly good, okay?! You try staying focused while getting smothered in feathers and magic. And what else am I supposed to do with my back to her?"

Typical interservice rivalry.

They had finally ended up in the dining area. An alcove held a few scattered crates, shelves, and a fireplace beneath some porous rock. On the other side, a few chairs were distributed around a cracked wooden table, all mismatched in style.

Helianne sat in the fanciest looking one.

Before her was a bowl of brown mush and black specks, made of what looked to be biscuit crumbs, vegetable tops, and plenty of spices whipped into a stew.

Next to that was a cup of violet-tinged liquid, smelling sour and tasting tangy. In the absence of wine, a mixture of water and vinegar was the next best thing for tiding her thirst.

It was perfect, and although the heat had long subsided, the air was still filled with enough excellence to have her swallowing constantly.

The prime heat of the Dustian chilis, the pepperiness of the... well, Roesian peppers, and the sweetness of the lichens from the foothills of Spire. She imagined the caravan wolves to be under her rule, and her domain vast. How fitting it was for a dish to be prepared with ingredients from all parts of her realm!

Maybe someday.

Likewise, nothing was as impressive as a chef who made much with so little. Aster's equivalent act would've involved bathing her with no soaps and shampoos after a day's trek, which seemed less palatable. Maybe this was what he was fretting about earlier.

Nerine poked Aster in the nose. "Hah! I've washed plenty of plants. How many soaps have you brewed?"

"And how many vegetables have you harvested, swamp-wolf?" In retaliation, Aster brushed his tail across her face.

It was fascinating when they were ascending the cave, but now the entertainment needed enhancement.

"Enough! A queen's servants shouldn't be fighting like this." Damn, that stew really hit the spot. The spices left a trail of fuzzies everywhere it went.

She dragged the werewolves by their gold collars to the opposite side of the table. Her eyes were eager as she spread her legs and pointed to the ground. "On your knees here. Both of you."

They crawled under the table, taking a side between her legs before her magic guided their heads closer, closer, and closer until their cheeks squished together.

As their breaths fogged the plumed crotch before them, their eyes feasted upon the impending feathers that their mouths were meant to serve.

Helianne shimmered her magic across their heads, teasing their scalps. "Now spread and lick."

They were getting along much better now. Each servant hooked their outer arm over her thigh, and their fingers went to work sifting, peeling, and whisking away the outer layer of feathers. When their fingers dug into her again, they spread her fluffy underlayer, and the harpy shivered as their breaths reached deep and bare.

Then they went to work.

Two pairs of werewolf tongues wrestled, lapped, and flitted about her nethers. They were large, rough appendages meant for cleaning meat off of bones. And pleasing queens.

Every shared skim across her clit and hood hollowed and convulsed her abdomen for several seconds as a breath forced out of her, and every wiggling shim against her entrance sucked a breath in.

When one teased her clit while the other teased her hole at the same time, her breath became trapped in her throat.

Her spine wriggled like a lamia as fervor dripped out of her.

Oh, how perfect things were. Aster had just been trained at the pool, and Nerine... well, not surprising a girl would know how to please a lady. It was good they had to make things up to her, because the difference between fingers and tongues was like...

Like... like werewolves...

And... uhmmm... the other kind of werewolves. Yeah, those big, sharp, furry ones that they'd tell fledglings about to keep them in the nest!

With her body properly attended to, she returned to the other pleasantry of life, and devoured another globule of stew. It had presence, lingering on her tongue with a rich and spicy aftertaste whose pungent heat made the dish feel like Nerine had served it fresh from the stove, and the trace sweetness brought a sense of longing for Spire.

The good parts of that place, anyway.

Another globule held a chunk of biscuit, which was the star of the meal. Soaked for a considerable amount of time, it carried the flavors of the vegetable broth well, and its rough, chewy texture made for quite the illusionary meat.

Meat. No, not fish or sea-bugs. Fleshed, full-bodied meat. Here, its fresh form spoiled too quickly for it to have been worth stocking by the merchants. Fauna being expensive to begin with in the barren canyon, the cost of a pound of its desiccated counterpart would've filled a full sack of biscuits, and the harpy's treasury was not infinite.

This was as good as it could get.

The musk from the werewolves' work below mingled with the flavors of the stew above, and the resulting union of scents lightened her. Just what kind of effect did it have on her servants' more sensitive noses...?

A spiced breath left the queen as her servants' soaked tongues licked deeply and coarsely against her. How kind of them to synchronize now. Their combined thicker and wider attempt started at the base of her slit, bunched her flesh as it roughly ascended, and then flicked her clit before wedging and squirming between it and her throbbing hood.

Her talons curled into the sandy ground, each grasping a helping of sand that curled her further as the grainy sensation drained through her claws.

Their tongues were fiery, and each graze into and against her flesh dripped fluids into their maws. While staring at the harpy throughout their care with those adorable eyes, they'd swallow their prey after every carve, and their cheeks increasingly kindled her aching thighs.

Curving her body, she peeked at their wavering loincloths. Aster's had protruded too much for it to have been gravity, and Nerine's had far too many trickles underneath for it to have been sweat. Despite that, their wills were iron, and their efforts remained on her thighs and nethers as they increasingly splotched the ground beneath them.

It wasn't often they'd collaborate so well. No fighting, no competing, no arguing, just two servants working to please Her Majesty as best and selflessly as they could. Their tails were intertwined too—something she'd never seen before. Perhaps in such trying times, they found solace in each other.

Or... not.

As soon as they caught her glance, they untangled themselves before boring their tongues deeper into her. Now they swayed their tails to opposite sides as if one repelled the other.

Her wingtip ran across the row of fluffy ears atop their heads before scratching the wolf girl's scalp. The edged teasing they had offered the harpy was nice, but it was time for release.

"Nerine, would you be a dear and attend to your queen's clit?"

Helianne did the same with the wolf girl's counterpart, tapping him on the back with a talon.

"Aster, remember that rough spot your fingers felt? Your queen wants your tongue to attend to that."

Pressed into her mound by a propped-up leg against their necks, her werewolves' mouths mumbled into her feathers before shifting.

Nerine was the first to move, dragging her lips upward across the harpy's flesh. The smooth texture squeaked against Helianne, and her grounded talon raked the earth. The wolf girl kissed and kissed her nub and hood as her other hand's fingers joined the tangle to spread her further. Each peck was sloppier than the last in effort, in connected juices, and in spittle.

Aster descended before lapping at her entrance. It was a tight squeeze with his temple pressed into his counterpart's cheek, but he managed. Their combined determination kept their heads stilled on her as his licks intensified in both depth and rate, making the harpy squirm in her seat.

The distance between the wolf girl's lips and Helianne's body diminished in every embrace until the gap was completely closed. Kisses turned into suckles that drew her nub and roof into the werewolf's maw. Nerine's tongue made quick sweeps against her exposed flesh until it snapped back out with a regal sigh and the cycle repeated.

Helianne oozed plenty throughout the upper werewolf's motions, all to be cleaned up by the lower werewolf. The wolf boy's swallows started out small and occasional, becoming more grand and persistent as time went on.

Aided by the increased slickness, his distance closed as well, first with rough laps against her folds, and then with licks that wedged his tongue inside her. Soon his lips were flush against hers, and his tongue no longer left her, instead flicking across her insides from the base of her tunnel to the top.

The harpy's clit buzzed in Nerine's mouth, and her flesh wrung Aster's tongue for all of its saliva. Panting like a werewolf herself, she shuffled her hips forward and back, trying to get more of her nethers into her servants' place of worship.

A peasantly grunt echoed through the cave as the harpy's legs jumped, bumping the table and nearly spoiling her supper.

After a last kiss of her flesh, Nerine sucked hard on her, stretching and drawing her deep into her maw in one continuous breath. Sharp teeth nibbled and grazed across her clit, shimmying sharp spikes of pain and pleasure up her spine that ended in a moan.

The harpy had grown so tight around Aster's tongue that she had forced his organ against the top of her tunnel. There, his tongue pumped in and out of her like a tentacle, grinding his bumpy taste buds into her special spot and sending bliss cascading back down her spine and out of her like an undammed river. His swallows couldn't catch up, and so his lips, cheeks, and chin became soaked with his queen's essence.

The wolf girl must've sensed the musky heat and the distress beneath her, for she moved lower until she too was ingesting her well-deserved share of her mistress's juices. Aster's tongue slipped out of the harpy, and they both alternated licks against her folds, each one gathering plenty of lust to be slurped and swallowed into their once-barren stomachs.

Shlick, shlick, shlick, they endlessly went, and citrusy, earthy musk plumed into her lungs as the rosy queen watched her servants' eyes upon her, like two pets seeking acknowledgement from their owner. She resisted the urge to tilt her head back and break the connection, so only the occasional sprayed gush broke their sight, but even then they'd rebind soon after.

Their tongues shared a final dribble equally, and they swallowed in unison before pressing their lips to her flesh and surrounding feathers to imbibe themselves in her residual essence. It didn't take long for her fluff to be damp, stained by werewolf saliva and nothing else.

"Her Majesty is... very pleased." Helianne could see their faces light up.

As the two werewolves made blushed pants, she brought a wing to their heads and rubbed them down, tarnishing their hair. Their ears would pop right back up as soon as her feathers shifted off of them, twitching while they prepared to be petted once more.

Wind whooshed behind them as their tails swished back and forth like metronomes. Fluids thick and thin dripped from beneath their loincloths, gathering on the sand in small shiny pools that eventually joined.

Her servants watched with wide eyes and grumbling bellies as Helianne finished the stew and then the posca. A cloth napkin patted down her face as she rubbed the edge of her wing across the back of her neck. That really hit the spot.

For her only.

Although they'd be relieved with tomorrow's grocery runback, it didn't feel right leaving them on the edge of hungering lust and lusting hunger for the night. Especially after all the royal duties they had so sincerely and selflessly fulfilled.

"Such good and loyal servants deserve to be cared for too, don't you agree?"

They nodded together.

If only she had something to offer them in return... Helianne rubbed her chin as she looked around, down at the werewolves, and then at herself.

Maybe, just maybe, she'd be able to...

No, the harpy was not laying any eggs; those only came in the mornings, anyway.

She had something much better and familiar for her finest werewolves.

5

Oblige

The evening turned to night as the sand turned cool beneath their feet. Luckily, they had only suffered on the walk to the bedroom. Layers and layers of mismatched cloth and fur shrouded the ground there, giving it a cloud-like feeling.

Inspired by her time in Spire, a hollow in the middle of a pile served as a nest for the three. Here her bare body was reclined at a perfect angle against its silken walls as she made calm breaths, drifting off into...

Nowhere.

Her equally bare servants were rather noisy eaters... or drinkers, in this case, and the sensation was rather distracting. Physically and mentally.

The harpy's servants straddled her feathered thighs as each of their cute faces dimpled a breast. The werewolves' hands kneaded the sides of them, extending their warmth into her chest and encouraging a steady flow of sustenance. Both were giving her that same melting look from before as they slurped from her.

Every so often they'd give her swollen nipples a deep draw, and pale heat would rush from her body onto their lapping tongues. The texture was rough on her private chambers, and it was equally rough on her storehouses, bringing forth murmurs and shivers from the queen as her loins simmered.

Each helping from her was as ample as the last, and they swallowed and sucked quickly, perhaps not wanting her luscious taste to dilute on their taste buds. Meant for chicks to build up fat quickly to survive the mountainous chill, her fare was thick and creamy.

During those moments, when her nourishment flowed and their bodies drank uninterrupted, she felt truly connected to their bodies as if they were of one existence cycling something vital like blood. As for the primality of all of it...

There was something heavenly, delightful, and right in watching them feast on this part of her. Eggs and nether-juices were one thing, but a harpy's milk was something special for someone special, like nestlings in need of growth. In some way, they fulfilled that purpose, and under her care, they'd grown into strong and dutiful servants who would continue to grow.

Her body had reformed the nutrients within the stew, posca, and perhaps the morning's biscuits into the milk within her laden breasts. Her werewolves would consume it, and that part of her would flow into their bellies before being digested and distributed within their own bodies, whether that be their bones, muscles, or even their adorable ears and tails.

Ahhh... she sucked in a breath as her talons twitched. The werewolves on her were a nice blanket against the nightly cold, but now the harpy was boiling beneath them, and her lower feathers were dampening.

It wouldn't be fair to attend to herself now, considering how well her servants had just pleased her.

And just as their tails and ears waggled in their own ways, they fed from her differently, too.

Aster drank and drank, whereas Nerine broke away from the harpy every so often to examine her own chest and then that of Helianne's. Her first attempts were subtle, involving just her eyes, but as Aster received a blessing to squeeze the harpy's breast for ampler offerings, the wolfess too grew shameless and began exploring their chests.

The werewolves were smaller in every way compared to Helianne. With wide eyes, Nerine looked deep in thought, comparing the different sizes of their nipples, cleavages, and even circumferences with her fingers.

"Nerine, is something the matter?"

Raising her haunches, the wolf girl was trying to line up her breast with the harpy's when she froze. "Sorry, Mistress, I... rarely get to see you like this. You're so..." She took a deep breath. "...bloomed."

Maybe her servants should've switched roles once in a while.

"There's no shame in being smaller, you know?" Helianne ran a wing across Nerine's fluttering ears. "Form fits function."

Aster chuckled into the harpy's breast.

"W-with all d-d-due respect, Your H-Highness, I... t-t-that wasn't what was on my mind!" The wolf girl was crimson as she straddled her thigh again.

It was unlike her to talk so fast and act all flustered.

"I *know* I'm wonderful, cute, beautiful... all those things, and I certainly don't need constant reassuring like—" Nerine's tail swatted Aster's rear. "—this insecure doofus here!"

Aster's tail swatted her right back, and he slightly rose. "Excuse me? You're the one who always—"

"Enough!" Holding a stern look, Helianne bopped both their heads with a wing. "Servants shouldn't be hungry and horny before bed." Her joined wings pushed their heads toward her until their lips were upon her nipples once more. "Drink. No more fighting."

After some mumbling, they both imbibed from her, and the harpy let out a half-pleasured and half-relieved sigh. While Helianne's loins were warm, theirs burned and dripped onto her.

All that one-sided work under the table, with no release. Poor werewolves.

She'd have to oblige them with more than just milk tonight.

Two violet wisps shimmered down their fronts, catching the werewolves' eyes and making them shuffle and make muffled giggles into her breasts as they continued to feed.

The harpy peeked at their waists before she aligned her mist with their nethers. It swirled around Nerine's drooling folds and Aster's equally drooling glans.

A wrinkle of her nose buried her magic inside both of them, clogging the exodus of pre and swelling their sexes.

Four arms embraced her tight as their abdomens flattened and squirmed against her. One wing hugged them back, while the other stroked their necks and heads. Their stifled moans echoed through her breasts, bringing the harpy close to laughter.

Eventually, their bodies adapted to the sensation, and they became as still as before. Their jagged teeth nibbled on her nubs between their licks, tensing the harpy's chest and jittering her magic within their bodies as she lost focus. That brought forth more nibbling.

A deep breath brought Helianne back in control, and she resumed creeping her presence through their bodies.

As she did so, the two werewolves ground their groins against her feathery thighs. Their ascent went against the grain, skimming her plumes against Aster's member and Nerine's slit until the fluffy down dug into his glans and her hood.

The descent freed her down from her servants' flesh with a cry, and their reascension into her velvety fluff flattened their lips against her nipples.

Helianne made it about an inch across the roof of Nerine's tunnel before the wolf girl's thighs clamped around the harpy's leg. Aster wasn't far behind, doing the same a few inches and seconds later.

Having her magic exactly where she wanted it, she gathered, built, and swirled her sorcery around those spots, making her servants tense and purr.

The harpy lifted her wing slightly, snooping on her quivering werewolves. "Hold hands and apologize."

Shuffles and shlicks sounded from beneath as their hands found one another and joined in the muggy space.

A trail of milk and spit connected Nerine's mouth to the harpy's nipple as her head jerked toward Aster. "I-I'm... I'm sorry for saying all those things...!"

Every part of Aster was twitching while he swallowed and turned to his equal. "And I'm sorry too! You're a wonderful friend and mentor!"

Helianne patted her werewolves on the head. "Now both of you count to three. And keep holding hands."

"One..."

Their unified hands were taut as they shook.

"Two..."

Their free hands clung to her back tight, and their claws dug in, nearly piercing her skin.

"T-three!"

Cheek to cheek, their heads slid into her cleavage, parting it as her magic unraveled within their flesh.

Her telekinesis vibrated, razed, and wrung their special spots simultaneously, and in an instant both werewolves were clinging to her and squirming in bliss as their holes squeezed against her magic with matching cadences.

They thrust so intensely that their pelvises slammed into the harpy's hip bones at every peak. They spewed, leaked, and twitched their fluids all over her feathers and skin, making a stringy, sticky mess across them.

Or so their bodies thought.

While their expulsions were strong, her magic was stronger, and their come stayed put, keeping their climaxes dry as the watery liquids prodded at a barrier that refused to give. Their come welled up within, rushing and swirling before that special spot with every spasm until dwindling to mere trickles.

Then there were no more reinforcements, and nor would there be any already present.

Her magic eased deeper, pushing the fluids back as her werewolves continued to clutch her tighter and tighter.

Sweat trickled from the harpy's temples as she stuck her tongue out and closed her eyes, focusing on the two very different anatomies before her.

Pressure built as their confused flesh tried so, so hard to expel what was meant to be expelled against her royal decree. A final lurch of her magic flushed their fevered flows to whence they came, and the pressure and potential mess was no more as Helianne's element dispersed.

"Thank you... Mistress..." The duo's breaths shined her cleavage one last time before they rolled off of her with relaxed bodies. Matching rhythms, their ears and tails continued to throb and pulse a few more times.

Ten claw-induced welts swelled with a tingling pain on the harpy's back like miniature bites. She imagined their hands' knuckles felt the same way. With how cute they looked exhausted, it was another thing she'd just have to overlook.

Helianne dragged the two werewolves closer until their heads were resting on her upper bosom—one above each breast—and facing each other. There, her servants murmured and shuffled as her magic reunited their hands. As their fingers finished intertwining, her wings closed in, blanketing them against their queen.

The shared warmth beneath her feathers felled the queen and her servants into slumber, and her heartbeats stilled with theirs as dreams overtook the day's worries.

About the Author

I write erotic fantasy stories featuring monster girls.

Enjoy reading about voracious succubus tails, slime-girl clone harems, fluffy harpy wings, and much, much more. Nothing excites me more than exotic body parts and fantastical abilities being used in naughty ways, especially when there's an assertive monster girl taking charge.

Follow me on these platforms:

Website | cithrel.com
Newsletter | cithrel.com/newsletter
Twitter | twitter.com/cithrel
Goodreads | goodreads.com/cithrel

Join the Newsletter

Join my mailing list to stay updated with what I'm working on: cithrel.com/newsletter

As thanks for signing up, you'll also receive **a free digital copy of *Succubus With Benefits 1.5***, a book that isn't available anywhere else!

The story takes place right after the events of the first book. It features sensual bathing, a hands-on investigation into succubus anatomy, and a very lewd cover illustration.

Also by Cithrel

If you enjoyed the story, consider leaving a review and exploring another monstrous tale. Your support is always appreciated!

A very experienced succubus seduces her very innocent summoner.

ALSO BY CITHREL

A newsletter-exclusive freebie! The day after, a succubus helps her master come to terms with his new desires.

An elf finds comfort in her water elemental. Literally.

Printed in Great Britain
by Amazon